Moo!

First published in 2003 by
Franklin Watts
338 Euston Road
London
NW1 3BH

Franklin Watts Australia
Level 17/207 Kent Street
Sydney
NSW 2000

A CIP catalogue record for this book is available
from the British Library.

ISBN 978 0 7496 5332 3

Series Editor: Jackie Hamley
Series Advisor: Dr Barrie Wade
Cover Design: Jason Anscomb
Design: Peter Scoulding

Printed in China

Franklin Watts is a division of
Hachette Children's Books,
an Hachette Livre UK company
www.hachettelivre.co.uk

Moo!

by Penny Dolan and Melanie Sharp

FRANKLIN WATTS
LONDON•SYDNEY

Big Bill had three cows: Daisy,
Buttercup and Cowslip.

In winter, they munched cow-feed in the barn.

In summer, they munched grass in the meadow.

Each morning, Bill took his three cows to the milking shed.

"Whisha-whisha-whisha!" went the milking machine, day after day. "Whisha-whisha-whisha!"

Daisy, Buttercup and Cowslip were really fed up with that sound.

Each week, Frank brought his tanker lorry to collect the milk. Big Bill and Frank enjoyed a chat while the tanker filled up.

One day, Frank looked worried. "Your cows aren't giving enough milk any more. I'll have to stop bringing my tanker," he said.

"You can't!" said Big Bill. "Without your tanker, I can't sell my milk!"

"I'm sorry," said Frank. "But the next trip might be my last."

Big Bill looked at his cows. "What am I going to do?" he said.

"Moo!" said Daisy.

"Moo!" said Buttercup.

"Moo!" said Cowslip.

The next morning, Big Bill felt so
sad that he stayed in bed.

His wife Millie went to the milking
shed instead.

As Millie stood by the milking
machine she sang, "Tra-la-la!
TRA-LA-LA!" Millie had
a strong voice.
"Moo?" said Daisy.
"Moo?" said
Buttercup.
"Moo, MOO!"
said Cowslip.
Somehow, there
was more milk
that day.

Millie was busy the next day, so
she left the children, Zack and Zoe,
to watch the milking machine.
They had good, strong voices, too.

"Hey, hey, yeah, YEAH!" they sang.

"Moo?" said Daisy.

"Moo?" said Buttercup.

"Moo, moo, MOO!" said Cowslip.

"Guess what? The cows made more milk today!" Zack and Zoe told Big Bill, proudly.

"Why's that?" asked Big Bill.

Zack and Zoe laughed and whispered in his ear. Suddenly, Big Bill gave an enormous grin.

The next morning, Big Bill took his three cows to the milking shed.

"Whisha-whisha-whisha!
Whisha-whisha-whisha!"
went the milking machine.

Then Big Bill took out his guitar.

"KERRANG-TWANG-TWANG!"

He sang and he danced.

He rocked and he bopped.

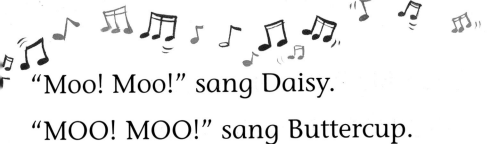

"Moo! Moo!" sang Daisy.

"MOO! MOO!" sang Buttercup.

"MOO! MOO! MOO!" sang Cowslip.

They loved Big Bill's music.

The three cows gave more milk
than they had ever done before.

Later, Daisy, Buttercup and Cowslip
bopped back to their meadow.

"Wow!" said Frank, as he checked his tanker. "There's lots more milk. Everything's fine again! What's your secret, Big Bill?"

"Just MOOsic!" chuckled Bill.

"Plenty of MOOsic!"

30

Hopscotch has been specially designed to fit the requirements of the Literacy Framework. It offers real books by top authors and illustrators for children developing their reading skills.

Marvin, the Blue Pig
ISBN 978 0 7496 4619 6

Plip and Plop
ISBN 978 0 7496 4620 2

The Queen's Dragon
ISBN 978 0 7496 4618 9

Flora McQuack
ISBN 978 0 7496 4621 9

Willie the Whale
ISBN 978 0 7496 4623 3

Naughty Nancy
ISBN 978 0 7496 4622 6

Run!
ISBN 978 0 7496 4705 6

The Playground Snake
ISBN 978 0 7496 4706 3

"Sausages!"
ISBN 978 0 7496 4707 0

Bear in Town
ISBN 978 0 7496 5875 5

Pippin's Big Jump
ISBN 978 0 7496 4710 0

Whose Birthday Is It?
ISBN 978 0 7496 4709 4

The Princess and
the Frog
ISBN 978 0 7496 5129 9

Flynn Flies High
ISBN 978 0 7496 5130 5

Clever Cat
ISBN 978 0 7496 5131 2

Moo!
ISBN 978 0 7496 5332 3

Izzie's Idea
ISBN 978 0 7496 5334 7

Roly-poly Rice Ball
ISBN 978 0 7496 5333 0

I Can't Stand It!
ISBN 978 0 7496 5765 9

Cockerel's Big Egg
ISBN 978 0 7496 5767 3

How to Teach a Dragon
Manners
ISBN 978 0 7496 5873 1

The Truth about those
Billy Goats
ISBN 978 0 7496 5766 6

Marlowe's Mum and
the Tree House
ISBN 978 0 7496 5874 8

The Truth about
Hansel and Gretel
ISBN 978 0 7496 4708 7

The Best Den Ever
ISBN 978 0 7496 5876 2

ADVENTURES

Aladdin and the Lamp
ISBN 978 0 7496 6692 7

Blackbeard the Pirate
ISBN 978 0 7496 6690 3

George and the Dragon
ISBN 978 0 7496 6691 0

Jack the Giant-Killer
ISBN 978 0 7496 6693 4

TALES OF KING ARTHUR

1. The Sword in the Stone
ISBN 978 0 7496 6694 1

2. Arthur the King
ISBN 978 0 7496 6695 8

3. The Round Table
ISBN 978 0 7496 6697 2

4. Sir Lancelot and
the Ice Castle
ISBN 978 0 7496 6698 9

TALES OF ROBIN HOOD

Robin and the Knight
ISBN 978 0 7496 6699 6

Robin and the Monk
ISBN 978 0 7496 6700 9

Robin and the Silver Arrow
ISBN 978 0 7496 6703 0

Robin and the Friar
ISBN 978 0 7496 6702 3

FAIRY TALES

The Emperor's New Clothes
ISBN 978 0 7496 7421 2

Cinderella
ISBN 978 0 7496 7417 5

Snow White
ISBN 978 0 7496 7418 2

Jack and the Beanstalk
ISBN 978 0 7496 7422 9

The Three Billy Goats Gruff
ISBN 978 0 7496 7420 5

The Pied Piper of Hamelin
ISBN 978 0 7496 7419 9

Goldilocks and the
Three Bears
ISBN 978 0 7496 7897 5 *
ISBN 978 0 7496 7903 3

Hansel and Gretel
ISBN 978 0 7496 7898 2 *
ISBN 978 0 7496 7904 0

The Three Little Pigs
ISBN 978 0 7496 7899 9 *
ISBN 978 0 7496 7905 7

Rapunzel
ISBN 978 0 7496 7900 2 *
ISBN 978 0 7496 7906 4

Little Red Riding Hood
ISBN 978 0 7496 7901 9 *
ISBN 978 0 7496 7907 1

Rumpelstiltskin
ISBN 978 0 7496 7902 6*
ISBN 978 0 7496 7908 8

Also look out for
Hopscotch Histories and
Hopscotch Myths!

* hardback